LULU the Tiger

Cupcakes for Drums

ANN LEE

Lulu the Tiger loves to rock and roll.
Music delights and tickles her soul.
Drumbeats cause her to swing and sway.
She taps her fingers to the beat every day.

"Look at Lulu tapping her fingers and thumbs."
Eddy Elephant says, "She needs a big set of drums."

"A drum set?" Lulu cries. "Yes, please!
Then I could drum all day with ease.
I just really hope that my dad agrees."

Lulu asks her dad, "Can I have a drum set?"
"Sure, if you help pay for them," Dad says. "You bet."

Lulu doesn't have money,
and drums cost a lot.
Gregory Giraffe visits and says,
"I have a thought.

What if we make yummy cupcakes to sell?"
"Great idea!" says Lulu.
"And lemonade as well."

They run to the kitchen.
Lulu can't wait to start.
Adding decorations is her favorite part.
She pulls out all the toppings she can find.
Candy and sprinkles, nuts of every kind.

Gregory feels like his head is spinning. "Slow down," he says. "Let's start at the beginning.

Before we make batter,
let's turn on the oven.
Then get out the pans that
we use to make muffins."

"Now we need a big bowl, cane sugar, and eggs."

Lulu dashes to bring them
and tangles her legs.

The eggs go flying and land
with a splatter.

"Oh, no!" Lulu cries. "Now
we can't make the batter."

"We can use applesauce."
Gregory tries not to frown.
"I know you're excited, Lulu,
but let's just calm down."

Lulu is more careful getting other supplies.
She cleans up the eggs so that nobody slides.

Gregory says, "Mix the applesauce, sugar, butter, and flour. Add the milk and stir well using lots of arm power."

Lulu and Gregory mix batters of all flavors.
They add chocolate, vanilla,
and cherry to savor.
Lulu pours them in pans and starts
the oven clock.
"Yum! I know these will sell.
Soon we'll be ready to rock!"

They make fresh lemonade with lemons, sugar, and water.
Lulu's dad comes in to check on his daughter.

He says, "Oooh, it smells like something yummy is baking. Looks like you've been busy. What are you making?"

Ding goes the oven. The cupcakes are done!
"There's your answer,"
Gregory says. "Now comes the fun."
"It's time to add frosting. What a delight!"

They smear on four colors:
red, brown, pink, and white.
Dad leaves the kids to decorate the cupcakes.
Lulu shakes on the sprinkles, nuts,
and coconut flakes.

When the cupcakes are ready,
the two head outside.

They set up a stand and
smile at it with pride.

All profits
for drums

Then they make a big sign
to draw in a crowd.
"Yummy cupcakes for sale!"
Lulu shouts out loud.

They try to be patient, since business takes time,

but their cupcakes are yummy, and soon there's a big line!

Gregory adds up the prices as customers pay.

Lulu hands them their cupcakes and says, "Have a great day!"

Hal Hippo and his family buy a whole bunch.
Zebra Zoe and her family get some for lunch.
Eddy Elephant buys much more than a few.
"Cupcakes are my favorite!" he says.
"Thank you two."

Gregory and Lulu sell all that they made.
The cupcakes are gone. So is the lemonade.
"Thanks for your help, Gregory,"
Lulu says with a smile.
"We made lots of money. Soon,
I'll be drumming in style."

Lulu sees her dad coming out the front door.
She shows him the money
and they head to the store.

Lulu tries out the drum sets.
There are so many!
"I love them all," she says.
"I'd be glad to have any."
She picks out her favorite
and counts out the money.
Her dad says,
"You earned this. I'm proud of you, honey."

Back at home,
Lulu plays her new drums in the yard.
"Wow!" Gregory says.
"It was worth working hard."

There are even two cymbals
for Gregory to play.
Now they rock and roll to the beat every day!

Enjoyed your copy of
LULU the Tiger Cupcakes
for Drums?

Please find the next series of LULU the Tiger Adventures;

LULU the Tiger and the Missing Shoes

on www.amzn.com/B08NWC9TP7

Special GIFT for you.
LULU's Activity book can be downloaded here;

https://BookHip.com/JBXNLS

Tigertastic ACTIVITY book

from

Pawesome LULU the Tiger

Applesauce cupcakes with butter frosting

Cupcakes

1/3 cup butter, softened
3/4 cup sugar
Two large eggs. Room temperature
Vanilla from 1 pod
1-1/3 cups all-purpose flour
One teaspoon baking powder
1/2 teaspoon baking soda
1/3 teaspoon salt
1 teaspoon ground cinnamon
1/4 teaspoon of other spices you like (nutmeg, cloves)
3/4 cup applesauce

1) Make sure all ingredients are at room temperature.
2) In a large bowl, cream butter and sugar.
3) Add eggs, 1 at a time, beating well after each addition. Beat in vanilla.
4) Combine dry ingredients; add to creamed mixture alternately with applesauce.
5) Fill greased or paper-lined muffin cups two-thirds full.
6) Bake at 350°F for 25 minutes or until a toothpick inserted in the center comes out clean.
7) Cool for 10 minutes before removing to a wire rack. Frost cooled cupcakes.

Frosting

1/2 cup butter (do not use margarine)
1/4 cup cream cheese
4 cups powdered sugar
2 teaspoons vanilla extract
3 to 4 tablespoons milk

1) In a 3-quart saucepan, melt butter over medium heat.
2) Cook 3 to 5 minutes, continually stirring and watching closely, until butter begins to turn golden (butter will get foamy and bubble.)
3) Remove from heat.
4) Cool 15-20 minutes.
5) With an electric hand mixer or kitchen aid on low speed, beat in powdered sugar, vanilla, cream cheese, and enough milk until frosting is smooth and desired, spreading consistency, adding 1 or 2 more teaspoons milk, if necessary.
6) Spread frosting on cooled cupcakes or use a pastry bag (if frosting begins to harden, stir in an additional tespoon of milk). Sprinkle it with chocolate, chopped almonds, dry fruits.

Want a free book?

Please get your copy of
The Best Color of All at:

https://bit.ly/2LeEUMn

About author

Ann Lee is an author and mother. Her children are the joy of her life and the inspiration for her writing. She decided early on that learning how to cook was not only an excellent way to stay healthy but fundamental for her children as they grow up.

Lulu the Tiger Cupcakes for Drums is her fifth book in the Cooking Adventures series, where she combines her imagination with teaching children how to cook.

More information about Ann and her books can be found at luluthetiger.com.

Printed in Great Britain
by Amazon

18151515R00025